Trolls on Hols

by Alan MacDonald

illustrations by Mark Beech

BLOOMSBURY

PRIDDLES: Roger, Jackie and Warren
Description: 'Pasty-faced peeples'
Likes: Peace and quiet
Dislikes: Trolls

Trolls on Hols

MR TROLL: Egbert / Eggy
Description : Tall, dark
and scaresome
Likes: Roaring, tromping,
hiding under bridges.

MRS TROLL: Nora
Description: Gorgeous
(ask Mr Troll)
Likes: Huggles and Kisses,
caves, the dark

ULRIK TROLL
Description: Big for his age
Likes: Smells, singing,
Rockball.

GOAT
Description:
Strong-smelling,
beardy beast
Likes: Mountains, grass
Dislikes: Being eaten

For the brilliant Kate Shaw
who believed in trolls – A.M.

To my sister Janet – M.B.

First published in Great Britain in 2007 by Bloomsbury Publishing Plc,
36 Soho Square, London, W1D 3QY

Text copyright © Alan MacDonald 2007
Illustrations copyright © Mark Beech 2007

A CIP catalogue record of this book is available from the British Library

ISBN 978 07475 8630 2

Printed in Great Britain by Clays Ltd, St Ives Plc

10 9 8 7 6 5 4 3 2 1

All papers used by Bloomsbury Publishing are natural, recyclable products made from
wood grown in well-managed forests. The manufacturing processes conform to the
environmental regulations of the country of origin.

www.bloomsbury.com/trolls

Going Vestless

I T WAS A HOT, sunny day at the start of the summer. At Number 10 Mountain View the Trolls were out in their back garden. Mrs Troll lazed in a deckchair, leafing through a magazine while she cooled her hairy feet in a bowl of water. Her husband had stripped off his vest and stood knee-deep in a hole that he was digging with his bare hands. Every now and then showers of earth flew in all directions. Ulrik lolled on the grass, staring at the sky. It was only three days since he had broken up from school and he had nothing to do.

'Mum,' he said.

'Yes, my ugglesome?'

'When are we going on holidays?'

'We *are* on holidays.'

'Yes, but I mean *real* holidays. Where you go somewhere.'

Mr Troll paused to wipe away a drip of sweat that hung from his snout. 'We could go to that stinksome hole under the high street, we haven't been there for weeks.'

Ulrik shook his head. 'That's a subway, Dad. I mean a proper holidays!'

Mr Troll climbed out of his hole and wiped his hands on his gigantic belly. He looked at his wife in bemusement. 'What the bogles is he talking about?'

'Ulrik's right. It's in my magazine,' said Mrs Troll. 'That's what peeples do in summer – go on their holidays.'

'Well, where is it then?' asked Mr Troll.

'What?'

'This holidays you want to go on.'

'How should I know? I've never gone on it!'

'Warren says it's the seasides,' explained Ulrik. 'You take a towel and you have to lie on it till you get really hot, then you tromp into the sea to cool down.'

Mr Troll snorted. 'Makes no sense. Why get all hot and blethered just so you can get cold again? Anyway, the sea is for fishes. Trolls don't belong in the sea. Caves and forests – that's where trolls live.'

'And houses,' Ulrik pointed out. 'We live in a house.'

'Yes, well, houses as well,' agreed Mr Troll. 'Caves and forests and houses.'

'But couldn't we go on a holidays, Dad? We've never been!'

Mrs Troll lifted her feet out of the bowl and waggled her toes.

'It might be nice, Eggy. Why don't we?'

'But I've just started making a piddling pool!' objected Mr Troll, pointing at the muddy hole he had dug.

'You can finish it when we come back.'

'Please, Dad!' begged Ulrik. 'Can we?'

Mr Troll sighed and picked up his vest. It was covered in dirt but he didn't mind since it was pretty filthy in the first place. 'We'll see,' he said. He studied the cover of Mrs Troll's magazine, which showed a sandy beach crowded with hundreds of people who seemed to be wearing only their pants.

'Hmm,' he said. 'So how do you get to this seasides?'

Ulrik didn't know, he'd never been to the sea. In fact, he'd never been much further than the high street. He'd been to Troll Mountain, of course – that's where they used to live before they moved to Biddlesden – but there was no sea back home, only mountains, forests and grey mist. He didn't know how far it was to the seasides. Could you walk there or did you have to catch a bus?

Mrs Troll had been thinking. 'What about that shop on the high street, Eggy? The Trouble Agents. I'm sure they do holidays.'

Mr Troll looked puzzled. 'You want to stay in a shop?'

'No,' said Mrs Troll. 'You ask the Trouble Agent and he finds you a holidays. It's like the supermarket only without the cornflakes.'

'Oh,' said Mr Troll. 'Well, if you want we can try it tomorrow.'

Next door Mrs Priddle stared out of her kitchen window while she chopped up carrots with more force than was strictly necessary.

'Look at him!' she tutted. 'It's disgusting!'

'What is?' asked her son Warren, hurrying over to look.

'That Mr Troll. Parading around in nothing but a tiny pair of shorts. As if I want to see that before my supper!'

'What's wrong with it? Dad sometimes wears shorts,' Warren pointed out.

'Yes, but he's not a troll. Look at the size of that belly. The least he could do is cover it up.'

Warren stood on a chair to get a better look at Mr Troll's belly. It was true it was impressively big. Warren had seen Mr Troll's belly before, bulging beneath the filthy vest he always wore, but today it was on display to the world. It was a pale green with a forest of coarse dark hair that spread from his chest to his belly button. When Mr Troll walked his belly wobbled like a blancmange. Warren thought you could hold a party on it. If Mr Troll lay on his back you could use him as a bouncy castle.

The front door slammed.

'Roger, is that you? Come and see this!' called Mrs Priddle.

Mr Priddle came in humming to himself happily and planted a kiss on his wife's cheek.

'See what, my darling?' he asked.

'That!' said Mrs Priddle, pointing next door. 'Can you believe it?'

'Oh! He's not digging holes again?'

'It's not the holes that worry me,' said Mrs Priddle. 'Look what he's wearing!'

Mr Priddle peered out of the window. 'Shorts,' he said.

'He's practically naked! I've never seen anything so horrible in all my life.'

'Well, don't look,' said Mr Priddle.

'This is my kitchen, Roger. I'll look where I like. I'm not going to go round with my eyes shut just because that ugly brute can't be bothered to wear a vest! This could go on all summer. Before we know it they'll all be parading around the garden in their underwear!'

'Ugh! Mum!' said Warren, pulling a face.

'Well, aren't you going to speak to him?' demanded Mrs Priddle.

'You're the one who's offended. You speak to him,' replied Mr Priddle.

'How can I speak to him? He's not wearing a vest!'

'Never mind his vest!' said Mr Priddle. 'I've got something to show you. Both of you. Come out the front.'

'Why?' asked Mrs Priddle suspiciously.

'You'll see. It's a surprise.' Mr Priddle groaned.

'Oh Roger, you know I hate surprises!'

Mr Priddle forced his wife and son to shut their eyes and, holding them by the arm, he led them outside.

'All right. You can look now.'

They both opened their eyes. 'Oh my giddy bananas!' gasped Mrs Priddle.

'It's a caravan,' said Mr Priddle.

'I can see that, Roger. But what's it doing on our drive?'

'It's ours!' said Mr Priddle proudly. 'I bought it.'

The caravan was the colour of pale custard. It had lace curtains at the windows that might have been white in Queen Victoria's day.

Warren thought it was brilliant. 'Can we look inside?' he asked eagerly.

'Of course!' said Mr Priddle. 'Just be careful with the light switch – it needs fixing.'

He took them on a tour. It didn't take too long since the caravan only had three rooms – a tiny bedroom, a tinier bathroom, and a kitchen-cum-dining-cum-everything-else room.

'See?' said Mr Priddle. 'You fold away the table like this and you've got another bed.'

'And who's going to sleep on that?' asked Mrs Priddle, folding her arms.

'Well, us,' said Mr Priddle. 'When we're on holiday.'

Mrs Priddle pursed her lips. 'If you think I'm having my holiday in this, you're mistaken–'

'I like it, Dad!' shouted Warren from next door, where he was using the bed as a trampoline.

'You promised me we'd have a proper holiday this year,' said Mrs Priddle.

'And we will. What could be more fun than a caravan?'

'A hotel,' said Mrs Priddle. 'A five-star hotel with a view of the sea. And a swimming pool.'

'Yes, but –'

'And cooked breakfast!' shouted Warren from next door. 'Sausage, bacon and eggs!'

'Be quiet, Warren!' ordered Mr Priddle. 'Anyway, we can have all those things – the view, the swimming pool – they'll all be on the caravan site.'

Mrs Priddle narrowed her eyes. 'What caravan site?'

'Um . . . well. . .' Mr Priddle stammered, 'I mean, if we found one we liked.'

'Roger,' warned Mrs Priddle, 'if you've done something stupid I'm going to scream.'

Mr Priddle dug in his pocket and brought out a scrap of paper. This wasn't going as well as he'd hoped. 'It's not a caravan site, it's more of a farm, really. I found the advert in *Caravan and Camping*.

His wife snatched the paper off him and read it out.

Paradise View
Find paradise in sun-kissed Wales.
Sea views, natural swimming pool, tennis court
– everything for a holiday you'll never forget.
Caravans welcome. Pets and children extra.
Phone: Olwen Ogwen – Boggy Moor 657770

'Olwen Ogwen?' said Mrs Priddle. 'What kind of a name is that?'

'He's Welsh. Sounded a nice chap on the phone.'

'You've spoken to him already?'

'Well, yes I had to . . . when I um . . . booked the holiday.'

Mrs Priddle let out a piercing scream and kicked the folding bed. There was a twang as it collapsed.

'Don't worry,' said Mr Priddle, 'that can be fixed.'

The Joy of Caravans

THE NEXT MORNING the Trolls trooped into town to visit the Travel Agents. The sales assistant who greeted them was called Kelly. Ulrik knew this because she had a name badge on her bright blue jacket. She had very white teeth and bright pink nails and smelled of perfume. Ulrik moved his chair a bit closer to the desk so he could smell her better. He was curious about peeple's smells. Most trolls smelled much the same – mainly of earth and sweat and goat-meat, if that's what they'd had for breakfast – but

Ulrik had noticed peeples had different smells. Babies, for instance, smelled of sick while old ladies smelled of mints.

Kelly smiled with her dazzling white teeth. 'How can I help?'

'We want to go on a holidays,' said Mrs Troll.

'No problem,' smiled Kelly. 'What kind of holiday did you have in mind?'

'Well, not a subway,' said Mrs Troll. 'We've been to one of those.'

'We want somewhere with mountains,' said Mr Troll.

'And the seasides,' nodded Ulrik.

'Towels too. It's got to have towels,' added Mrs Troll.

Kelly's smile had faded and she was looking slightly confused. 'Towels?' she said.

'Yes, to sit on. We don't want sandy bits on our bottoms.'

'Well, no,' agreed Kelly. 'But generally most people take their own towels.'

Mrs Troll shook her head firmly. 'We don't have any.'

'No,' said Mr Troll. 'Trolls never wash – it takes away your stink.'

Kelly laughed, hoping this was a joke. They seemed to have got off the subject.

'So you're interested in a beach holiday?' she said.

'Is that at the seasides?' asked Mrs Troll.

'Well, yes, most beaches are.'

'Then that's what we want.'

'No problem, we've got plenty of choice. Have you thought where you'd like to go? Spain? America? The Greek Islands?'

'That sounds good. Can we walk there?' asked Mr Troll.

'Which?'

'The Goat Islands.'

'Um . . . Greek Islands. Not really. You'd need to fly.'

Mr Troll snorted. 'We're trolls, not ducky birds. How can we fly?'

Kelly glanced behind them. A queue of people were waiting.

'You don't have to go abroad,' she said. 'There are plenty of options at home. Where would you like to stay? In a hotel?'

Mr Troll leaned forward 'What about a cave?'

'A cave?'

'Yes, we'd like that,' agreed Mrs Troll. 'A nice stinksome cave.'

Kelly shook her head. 'I don't think we have any . . . um . . . cave holidays. If you want something cheaper, why don't you try camping or perhaps a caravan?'

'A carry-bag?'

'That's what Warren's going on!' said Ulrik eagerly. 'He told me his dad's bought a carry-van and they're going to Wales.'

'That sounds nice, Eggy,' said Mrs Troll. 'I've always wanted to see whales.'

Mr Troll wrinkled his snout. 'Big blubbery things.'

Kelly was busy tapping on her computer keyboard.

'What about this?' she said. 'Two weeks at Golden Sands Holiday Park in a luxury caravan.'

'Luxury. That sounds nice, Eggy,' said Mrs Troll.

'Uggsome!' said Ulrik. 'Can we go, Dad?'

Mr Troll considered. 'Does it have a piddling pool or do we have to dig our own?'

Kelly consulted her screen. 'Let's see . . . there's an outdoor swimming pool.'

'Then we'll go,' said Mr Troll. He'd had enough digging for one week.

Kelly tapped again. 'Lovely. That will be £599 if you go before August.'

The Trolls looked shocked. None of them had considered they might have to pay for a holiday. They assumed that Travel Agents were giving them away. Mrs Troll reached into her bag and brought out the sock she used as a purse. She peered inside – they definitely didn't have that much money.

'Let's talk to the Priddles,' she suggested. 'They've got a carry-thing.'

'So you don't want to book?' asked Kelly.

'No thanks,' said Mr Troll. 'Maybe we'll come back tomorrow.'

'Of course.' Kelly stood up and smiled with relief. Tomorrow was Sunday and thankfully they were closed.

Later that evening Mrs Priddle happened to glance out of her bedroom window.

'Roger!' she called downstairs. 'You better get outside. Mrs Troll's looking at your caravan.'

'Oh, good gravy!' cried Mr Priddle and hurried outside in his slippers. He found Mrs Troll with her snout jammed up against the back window.

'What do you think? A beauty, isn't she? I only

picked her up yesterday,' said Mr Priddle, modestly patting the side of his caravan.

'Has it got towels?' asked Mrs Troll.

'Well, yes, it's got everything,' said Mr Priddle. 'Want to have a look inside?'

Mrs Troll did. The caravan was a little on the small side and she had to duck low to fit through the door, but once inside she was enchanted with the cosy little room. Mr Priddle took her round, pointing out the cooker, the fridge-freezer, the shower and all the modern gadgets the caravan had to offer. Mrs Troll was especially impressed with the table that magically turned into a bed.

'So what do you think?' asked Mr Priddle.

'It's stinksome,' said Mrs Troll.

'Well, yes, I know it could do with a good clean.'

'No, don't spoil it. It's got a lovely stink.'

'Oh well . . . thanks,' said Mr Priddle.

'And you're going on this for your holidays?'

'Yes, we're off bright and early tomorrow to miss the traffic. It's quite a journey to Wales.'

'Yes, you only get them in the sea.' Mrs Troll nodded wisely. She looked around the caravan enviously. 'Ulrik has been begging us for a holidays, poor hairling. I wish we could go on a caravan.'

'Well, you should try it,' said Mr Priddle.

'Me?' said Mrs Troll.

'All of you. There's nothing to beat it. Go where you like, stay as long you please – with a caravan you're free as a bird. Who needs an expensive hotel when you've got everything you need right here?'

Mrs Troll had never thought of it that way before. 'Maybe you're right.'

'I am right. You should give it some thought,' urged Mr Priddle.

'Well, I will – if you're sure.'

'Sure? I'm positive! I think you'd love it.'

'All right. Thank you. I'll see what Eggy thinks.'

Mrs Troll's dark eyes were shining with delight and she suddenly hugged her neighbour.

Mr Priddle watched her go. She had seemed quite impressed with the caravan, though he had a nagging sense that they'd been talking about different things. What had she meant when she'd asked him if he was sure? Sure of what? He'd only meant they ought to consider buying a caravan of their own. So why had she acted as if he was doing them an enormous favour?

Mrs Priddle was waiting for her husband in the kitchen. 'Well, what did she want?'

'Nothing really – just a look round. Actually, we had quite a nice chat. Very keen on the caravan.'

'Huh!' snorted Mrs Priddle. 'When you live in a pigsty, anything looks good.'

'They're really quite friendly if you give them a chance,' said Mr Priddle.

Mrs Priddle clicked her tongue. 'Don't be ridiculous, Roger,' she said. 'The best thing about going away is we won't have to see them for two whole weeks.'

Next door at Number 10, Mrs Troll had reported the conversation to her husband.

'Are you sure?' he said.

'Of course I am, Eggy. He wants us to go on holidays with them!'

'Blunking bogles!' said Mr Troll. 'What did he say?'

'He said we should try it, all of us. He thinks we'd love it.'

Ulrik came into the kitchen. 'Love what, Mum?'

'A caravan holiday, hairling,' said Mrs Troll. 'The Priddles have asked us to go with them.'

'Uggsome!' said Ulrik. 'Are we going?'

Mrs Troll looked at Mr Troll. 'What do you think? Shall we, Eggy?'

Mr Troll picked at one of his fangs. 'Won't it be a bit squished? Six of us together in that tiddly tin can?'

'It's bigger inside than you'd think,' said Mrs Troll. 'It's got a table that turns into a bed. Why don't we, Eggy? No one's ever asked us on holidays before.'

Mr Troll thought it over. It was true they didn't have a caravan and the Priddles had a perfectly good one. This way too it wouldn't cost them any money.

'All right,' he said. 'We'll go!'

Ulrik gave a loud whoop and threw himself on his dad, wrestling him to the ground. A mock fight broke out, with the two of them growling and laughing.

Mrs Troll left them to it and bustled upstairs. If they were going to leave early in the morning, she'd have to start packing. In fact there was hardly any point in going to bed. An idea struck her. Why not give the Priddles a lovely surprise? They could move into the caravan tonight so they'd be all ready for the early start in the morning. She couldn't wait to see the look on Mr Priddle's face when he opened the door.

Paradise View

THE TROLLS SLEPT soundly through the journey, lulled by the sound of cars overtaking on the motorway. They were still dozing when the caravan pulled into a driveway by a signpost that said 'Paradise View'. The caravan rocked from side to side as it climbed a potholed track to the top of a hill. Mr Priddle parked and turned off the engine. He peered through the steady drizzle outside.

'Is this it?' asked Mrs Priddle. 'Where are all the other caravans?'

The Priddles got out and looked around, huddled under a golfing umbrella. Even Mr Priddle had to admit that Paradise View fell short of what he was expecting. A few sheep grazed in a field of scrubby grass. There was one rusty tap, a barn with a rickety roof, a grim-looking farmhouse and not much else. Crows cawed in the woods behind them. A man came out of the farmhouse and strode towards them with two sheepdogs trotting at his heels.

'Ah,' said Mr Priddle. 'This will be Ogwen.'

'Tell him,' his wife hissed. 'Tell him we don't want to stay.'

Farmer Ogwen stepped over a puddle. He had a face like a knobbly red potato. His cord trousers were tied at the waist with string and tucked into his muddy boots. Warren thought he looked more like a tramp than the owner of a caravan site.

The two dogs circled them, growling softly.

'Quiet, Fang! Down, Claw!' Ogwen barked. He smiled, revealing his two remaining teeth and held out a grubby hand.

'Olwen Ogwen. Don't worry about the dogs – they won't hurt you. Quiet, boys! Quiet, I said!'

The dogs ceased their growling but Warren kept close to the caravan just in case.

'You must be Widdle,' said the farmer. 'You found us all right then?'

'Yes. It's Priddle. Roger Priddle.'

'Oh, right you are. So you're on your holidays, are you? You'll like it here. Paradise on earth it is.'

'Ends of the earth more like,' muttered Mrs Priddle.

'Eh?' demanded Ogwen.

Standing close to the caravan, Warren could hear strange noises coming from inside.

'Dad!' he said.

'Not now, Warren – I'm talking. I was wondering, Mr Ogwen, where are all the other caravans?'

'Oh. Too early in the season,' said the farmer. 'Packed this will be in a couple of weeks. They'll be queuing right along the lane.'

Mrs Priddle tried to imagine the bare field crowded with happy holidaymakers but it was asking a lot of her imagination.

Mr Priddle looked around. 'The advert . . .' he began.

'You saw that, did you? Wrote that myself,' said Ogwen.

'But it mentioned a swimming pool. I can't see it.'

Farmer Ogwen pointed to the bottom of the hill. 'Down there – look. By the reeds.'

'That's a pond,' said Mrs Priddle, squinting into the rain.

'Yes, natural pool that is. Beautiful on a hot day. The cows love it.'

Mrs Priddle turned pale. 'Roger, say something,' she muttered.

'Um . . .' said Mr Priddle.

Warren, meanwhile, was listening. There was definitely something moving about in the caravan. Bumps and thumps and scrapes came from inside. 'Dad!' he said again.

'Not now, Warren!' snapped Mr Priddle. 'And the tennis court? Where's that?'

'Oh, that went last year. Sheep kept eating the grass. And there's the problem of droppings, see? Can't stop sheep doing what's natural, can you?'

Mrs Priddle gave a faint moan.

'But the view,' her husband ploughed on. 'Your advert promised a "sea view".'

'Well, there is!' smiled Ogwen, showing his two teeth. 'If you climb the hill on a clear day you can see it across the moor. Of course it's not clear now, mind – it's raining. Always rains on Boggy Moor.' He clapped his hands together, 'So, if that's all, I'll leave you to get settled in, shall I?'

He turned to go, but a loud knocking sound caught his attention.

'Someone in your caravan, is there?'

Mr Priddle glanced at his wife. 'No.'

'That's what I keep telling you!' said Warren. 'There *is* something. Listen!'

They all stood and listened. A loud thump came from inside the caravan and Mr Priddle took a step back. The handle of the door rattled as if someone was trying to get out. Mrs Priddle looked as if she might faint. They had been travelling for hours, they had come to a place run by a tooth-less madman – and now this.

'Better open the door, hadn't you?' said Ogwen.

Mr Priddle took a deep breath. He unlocked the door, turned the handle and leapt backwards as if he was releasing a caged lion. A hairy head appeared, blinking at them. Mr Troll was wearing his red Bermuda shorts and nothing else.

'Ah, Piddle,' he said, scratching under his arms. 'What's for breakfast?'

Mr Troll stepped out of the caravan into the drizzly rain, followed by Ulrik. Mrs Troll came next, wearing a flowing pink nightie, trimmed with silk bows.

'My stars!' said Ogwen. 'How many have you got in there?'

Mrs Priddle glared at her husband. 'Don't look at me!' said Mr Priddle. 'I had no idea!'

Ulrik was looking around. He had been expecting a sandy beach with waves lapping on the shore, but all he could see was a muddy field and a dozen sheep. He tugged at his mum's arm. 'Where's the seaside, Mum?'

'Never mind that!' said Mrs Priddle. 'What on earth are you doing here?'

Mrs Troll looked mystified. 'We're on holidays, same as you.'

'But you can't just turn up! You can't just move into our caravan, uninvited!'

'We *were* invited,' replied Mr Troll. 'He invited us.' He pointed a fat finger at Mr Priddle.

Mrs Priddle turned on her husband. 'Roger! You didn't!'

'Of course I didn't!'

'Don't tell fibwoppers. You did!' said Mrs Troll.

'No I didn't!'

'Oh yes you did!'

'Don't stop!' grinned Ogwen. 'This is better than a pantomime.'

'You said we should try a caravan holiday. You told me we'd love it,' said Mrs Troll.

'Yes, but I didn't mean come on holiday with us!'

'Didn't you?'

'No!'

'Then why did you invite us?'

Mr Priddle gave up – they were going round in circles. He should have known something like this would happen. It seemed the Trolls followed them around like bad luck.

'Well, this is marvellous,' said Mrs Priddle bitterly. 'Just wonderful!'

'Isn't it?' said Mr Troll, beaming. 'All of us together! On holidays.'

Farmer Ogwen had been making calculations. 'So there's six of you,' he said. 'You only said three on the phone. I'm afraid six is going to be extra.'

Mrs Priddle jumped to her feet. This was the last straw. 'There are not six of us,' she said. 'There is only room in this caravan for three.'

'Well, that's what I said,' agreed Mr Troll. 'So where are *you* going to sleep?'

Later that evening the Priddles sat round the table inside the caravan, drinking mugs of hot chocolate. Warren wiped the mist from the window beside him and looked out.

'They're still there,' he said.

'What are they doing?' asked Mr Priddle.

'Getting wet.'

Mr Priddle glanced at his wife. 'Don't look at me like that,' she said. 'There isn't any room.'

'But we can't leave them out there all night, Jackie. They'll catch their death.'

'You should have thought of that before you invited them.'

'For the last time, I didn't invite them!' cried Mr Priddle. 'It was all a mistake.'

Mrs Priddle glared back. 'If you ask me, this entire holiday was a mistake. This place should carry a health warning. I can't walk out the door without stepping in sheep muck, and as for that so-called swimming pool, the only things swimming in there are frogs and newts!'

Warren kept his nose pressed against the window. 'Do you think they will catch their death?' he asked.

'Warren!'

'I'm only asking. It might get cold tonight.'

'They're trolls,' said Mrs Priddle. 'They're used to the cold.'

There was a silence. Mrs Priddle drained the last of her hot chocolate. Warren and Mr Priddle gazed at her reproachfully. The rain fell harder, drumming on the roof.

'Oh, go on then,' sighed Mrs Priddle. 'I must be out of my mind.'

'I'll tell them,' said Mr Priddle. He took the golfing umbrella and went outside.

The Trolls came in and stood by the door. Rain dripped off them, collecting in puddles at their feet.

'Thank you,' said Mr Troll, shaking himself like a dog.

'It's only for one night,' warned Mrs Priddle. 'You'd better get out of those wet clothes.'

'Good idea,' said Mr Troll, pulling off his soggy vest.

'Not here!' shouted Mrs Priddle. 'Go in the bathroom and change. I'm afraid you'll all have to squash in one bed.'

'That's all right,' said Mrs Troll. 'We're used to squishing. We can squish in with you if you like.'

Mrs Priddle shuddered. 'Please, no! Just go to bed. Maybe in the morning we'll find this was all a nightmare.'

The Trolls retired and before long the only sound to be heard was the rumbling of Mr Troll's snores. Ulrik lay awake listening to the rain pattering on the roof. Holidays were quite different from what he'd imagined. You seemed to spend a lot of time arguing and getting wet. Still, tomorrow was a new day; maybe if it stopped raining they'd go to the seaside.

Painting Sheep

THE NEXT DAY the clouds had blown away and the sun shone in a clear, blue sky.

After a breakfast of scrambled eggs and burnt toast (Mr Priddle said the grill needed fixing) Ulrik and Warren asked if they could go off to explore by themselves.

The two of them wandered down the hill past the wood where the crows called to them. Ulrik could see Boggy Moor emerging from the morning mist. It looked wild and deserted, a bit like Troll Mountain, though obviously without the mountain.

'Let's play Hide and Seek,' Warren suggested.

'Is that the same as Roar and Seek?' asked Ulrik. 'I used to play that with my friends.'

'It's easy peasy. I hide and you've got to find me.'

'And when do you roar?'

'You don't roar!' said Warren impatiently. 'There's no roaring in this game, OK?'

'OK. But how am I meant to find you?'

Warren rolled his eyes. 'Look, it isn't complicated. You just close your eyes, count to fifty, then come and look for me. Got it?'

'Yes,' said Ulrik. 'Where will you be?'

'Arghhh!' cried Warren.

Ulrik frowned. 'I thought you said there wasn't any roaring.'

'Just shut your eyes and count!'

Ulrik did as he was told and counted to fifty out loud. When he opened his eyes he was alone. He scanned the hill, trying to guess where Warren would have gone. Apart from the barn and the woods there weren't many places to hide. He decided to try the barn first.

Pushing open the door, he breathed in the sweet smell of straw and muck. It smelled a bit like their house in Mountain View. At the far end of the barn someone was bending over, surrounded by sheep.

'Found you!' cried Ulrik.

But when the person turned round, it wasn't Ulrik. It was Farmer Ogwen, who gave him a gap-toothed smile. He was wearing the same shabby clothes as yesterday and he'd forgotten to shave.

'Hello,' said Ulrik. 'I was looking for Warren. Have you seen him?'

'Not in here.'

'We're playing Hide and Sneak. I've got to find him but roaring's not allowed.'

Ogwen raised one bushy eyebrow. 'Just as well. You might have scared me.'

Ulrik shrugged modestly. 'Dad says my roar's getting fiercer. I'm having lessons.'

'Good for you.'

Ulrik decided he liked Ogwen's soft, sing-song way of talking. Most people he met for the first time backed away as if he was going to bite them, but Ogwen seemed quite at ease. He went back to colouring one of the sheep with the blue marker in his hand.

'Aren't they meant to be white?' asked Ulrik.

'What's that then?'

'Sheeps. You're colouring them blue.'

The farmer chuckled to himself. 'Oh, not blue all over. That's my mark, see? Anyone finds this sheep, they'll see that blue mark and they'll know she belongs to me.'

'Oh, I see! Like my feetball socks,' said Ulrik.

'Are they blue?'

'No, they're red, but they've got my name inside, so peeples at school know they're mine.'

Ogwen nodded. 'Same thing. Sheep are like socks, always getting lost.' He gave Ulrik a wink. 'You want to give me a hand?'

Ulrik nodded. He liked colouring. They did it at school, though mostly on paper rather than sheep. Ogwen showed him how to make a large splodge on the sheep's fleece using the blue marker. Once he'd got the hang of it, he did several more. Some of the sheep had red spots, which Ogwen explained was a mistake that needed to be corrected. Ulrik was so involved in what he was doing that he didn't notice Warren come into the barn.

'Ulrik! I thought you were coming to look for me,' he complained.

Ulrik swung round. 'Oh, sorry, Warren. I forgot.'

'It's my fault,' said Ogwen. 'He's been helping me.'

Warren leaned on the side of the pen sulkily. 'I've been waiting for hours. You never would have seen me. I found this great place in the woods.'

Ogwen looked up sharply. 'The woods?'

'Yes,' said Warren. 'Why?'

'You don't want to go there. It's close to the moor. I should have warned you.'

'What's wrong with the moor?' asked Ulrik.

'Wrong? Surely you know about Boggy Moor?'

They both shook their heads. Ogwen beckoned them over with a grimy finger and lowered his voice. 'There's things happen on the moor, boys – bad things. No one goes there, not after dark. You take my advice.'

'Why?' asked Warren in an awed whisper. 'Why don't they go there?'

The farmer shook his head. 'Take it from me, it's not safe. You keep away from the moor. Keep away.'

He shook a bony finger in warning and then turned back to his sheep.

'What do you think he meant?' asked Ulrik as they left the barn.

'I don't know,' said Warren. 'He's probably just pulling our leg. Trying to scare us.'

'Yes,' said Ulrik. 'Probably.' He glanced back at the wood, and the bleak moor beyond.

'Anyway, I'm not scared,' said Warren.

'Nor me,' agreed Ulrik. The caravan was in sight now and they broke into a run.

Swimming Lessons

MR PRIDDLE SAID that since the sun was shining they should spend the day on the beach. He had hoped the Trolls might have other plans but it turned out they had no plans at all.

The six of them squashed into the Priddles' car, with Warren reluctantly forced to sit on Mrs Troll's lap since he was the smallest. Once at the beach car park, they unloaded their bags, buckets and spades and followed the steep path down to Sunny Bay.

Down at the beach Ulrik noticed that everyone stopped what they were doing to stare at the Trolls. Shouts and laughter died away on the air. People drew back to let them through, pointing and whispering among themselves.

Mr Priddle set down his bags by some rocks.

'Let's stop here,' he suggested. 'The tide's coming in.'

A little girl ran past and stopped in front of Ulrik. She pointed a chubby finger.

'Dad! Dad! It's the big bad beast!'

Ulrik bent down to give her his friendliest smile, but before he could say anything, the girl's dad came running and gathered her up in his arms.

Looking around, Ulrik saw people were beginning to desert the beach. Some gathered up their belongings while others panicked and simply left their towels and rugs behind as they fled. Within five minutes of their arrival the beach was empty except for the Trolls and the Priddles.

Mrs Troll stared open-mouthed. 'What's wrong with everyone?'

'It's you!' said Mrs Priddle. 'Didn't you see the way they looked at you?'

'Well, haven't they seen trolls before?'

'Of course they haven't! This is Wales.'

'But we weren't trying to fright anyone,' said Mr Troll. 'I haven't roared once.'

Mr Priddle looked up and down the deserted beach. 'Well, it looks like we've got the place to ourselves. We might as well enjoy it.'

He began to set up the windbreak, hammering the poles into the sand while his wife spread out three beach towels. Once this was done, the trolls watched in surprise as the Priddles began to undress, stripping off their tops and shorts.

Mrs Priddle caught them staring. 'Aren't you getting changed?'

'Are we, Mum?' asked Ulrik.

'If you want, my ugglesome,' said Mrs Troll. 'Maybe we should.'

She began unbuttoning the flowery summer dress she was wearing. Mr Troll shrugged and tugged his grubby vest over his head. He unzipped his shorts and kicked them off. He was about to take off his pants when Mrs Priddle stopped him.

'WAIT!' she screamed, turning pink. 'Aren't you wearing trunks?'

'Trunks?' said Mr Troll. He looked at his wife. 'Have we got trunks?'

'I don't think so, Eggy.'

'Then what are you going to wear?' demanded Mrs Priddle.

'Same as you. We'll go bareskin,' said Mrs Troll, stepping out of her dress.

'Bareskin? You can't walk around naked!' said Mrs Priddle. 'This is a beach – people are looking!'

'No they aren't. All the peeples ran away,' said Mr Troll.

'Well, I am a peeples . . . I mean, a person,' said Mrs Priddle. 'And if you haven't got swimsuits at least keep some clothes on!'

Mr Troll sighed and bent down to pick up his shorts. There was no pleasing peeples, he thought. First they told you to take off your clothes, then they wanted you to put them back on. In any case he couldn't see what all the fuss was about. Back home trolls went bareskin all the time.

Mrs Priddle had settled herself on her towel and was rubbing some kind of cream on her legs. Mrs

Troll watched enviously. She didn't have a towel to sit on and she didn't have any cream. She sat down next to Mrs Priddle and sniffed her legs. The cream smelled quite nice, like tinned peaches.

'Isn't there somewhere else you could sit?' asked Mrs Priddle, coldly.

'I haven't got a towel,' said Mrs Troll.

'Of course not. No towels, no swimsuits – anything else you didn't bring?'

'Legs cream,' said Mrs Troll, pointing at the tube in Mrs Priddle's hand.

'It's called suncream. You put it on to stop you burning. '

'Are you burning?' Mrs Troll looked above Mrs Priddle's head, checking for signs of smoke.

'No, because I always wear suncream. I've got delicate skin,' said Mrs Priddle, smoothing back her blonde hair. She sighed wearily. 'Look, if you want some, there's another tube in the bag.'

Mrs Troll rummaged in the Priddles' picnic bag. Under the sandwiches and crisps she found a large yellow tube which she assumed was the spare suncream. She squeezed a blob on to her hand. It was thick and yellow, though it didn't smell of peaches. She began to rub it on to her arms. 'Eggy!' she said. 'Can you rub some of this on my back?'

'What for?' asked Mr Troll.

'It's suncream – it stops you from burning. You should try some.'

Mr Troll sniffed the tube and pulled a face. 'Smells of eggs,' he said. He squeezed out a large blob and began to rub it on to his wife's hairy back. Warren, in the meantime, had changed into his swimming trunks and was waiting impatiently.

'Are you ready, Dad? I want to go for a swim!'

Mr Priddle groaned. 'Not yet! I've only just sat down.'

Mrs Priddle lay back on her beach towel and opened her book. 'Go and swim with him, Roger. The water looks lovely.'

Ulrik looked. It was true, the sun was sparkling and dancing on the waves.

'I've never swimmed in the sea,' he said a little nervously.

'Never?' said Warren.

'No. Dad says the sea is for fishes.'

Mrs Troll flicked off a wasp that was crawling up her thigh. 'That's because he's frighted of water.'

'I am not!' growled Mr Troll indignantly.

'You are, Eggy. You never go near it. Not since that time you got butted off a bridge by a billy goat.'

Mr Troll scowled. He didn't see the point of the seaside. There was nothing to chase and no one to roar at.

Mr Priddle adjusted the waist of his swimming trunks and took a few deep breaths. 'The best way is to run straight in,' he advised Ulrik. 'Don't paddle about in the shallows. Just take a deep breath and dive in. Copy me and you'll be fine.'

'OK, I'll try,' nodded Ulrik.

They ran down the beach. Ulrik was the first to reach the water and splashed in excitedly. A wave broke over his knees as he plunged in deeper. The water was as cold as ice. Mr Priddle jumped up and down shouting, 'Ahhh! Heee! Ha-hooo!'

'Ahhh! Heee! Ha-hoooo!' repeated Ulrik, anxious to do everything correctly. They were up to their waists now. Mr Priddle stretched out his arms and flapped them as if he was a pigeon preparing for take-off. 'Oh! Oh my . . . !' he gasped, but the rest was lost as a huge wave crashed over all three of them and Ulrik got a mouthful of salt water. When he could see again, he found he was on his own. Mr Priddle was wading back rapidly towards the beach, spluttering and coughing. Ulrik splashed after him excitedly. 'Uggsome!' he called. 'Did you see me? I swimmed!'

Back on the beach they found Mrs Troll performing an odd kind of dance. She shook her head, flapped her arms violently and slapped at her thighs.

'Do you have to do that?' complained Mrs Priddle. 'You're kicking sand on me.'

'I can't help it,' said Mrs Troll. 'It's these buzzle-bees – they're everywhere!'

Mrs Priddle put down her book. A cloud of insects hovered over Mrs Troll, buzzing angrily. 'They're not bees, they're wasps!' she yelped, leaping to her feet.

'Wisps?' said Mrs Troll.

'Wasps! Where did they come from?'

'I don't know,' said Mrs Troll, swatting the air furiously. 'But I wish they'd go back.'

Mrs Priddle noticed the yellow drips running down Mrs Troll's legs.

'What on earth is that?' she pointed.

'Suncream.'

Mrs Priddle saw the empty yellow tube lying on the sand and seized it. 'Wait! You didn't use this?'

'Yes, it was in the bag.'

'Not the picnic bag! That's mayonnaise! It's meant for the sandwiches!'

'What?' gasped Mrs Troll.

She rushed off towards the sea with the angry wasps buzzing after her. On the way she passed Ulrik, who stopped to watch his mum plunge into the waves, flapping her arms above her head. For a beginner, she seemed to be getting the hang of swimming.

Ten minutes later Mrs Troll sat shivering on the sand with a beach towel wrapped around her.

'How are you feeling now?' asked Mr Troll, sitting down beside her.

'Sore,' said Mrs Troll. 'I've been stinged all over.'

Mr Troll sniffed her shoulder. 'You still smell stinksome,' he said.

'Thank you, my lugly,' said Mrs Troll.

Warren and Ulrik had been trying to play football but the tide was coming in and the ball kept going in the sea.

'Mum, I'm hungry! Can't we get an ice cream?' whined Warren.

'I think that's a very good idea,' said Mrs Priddle. 'Why don't we all go to the café and have a nice cup of tea?'

Sunny Bay Café was a small wooden building just down the hill from the car park. Considering it was the holiday season it didn't seem to be very busy. The only customers were an elderly couple drinking coffee at a table in the corner. When they saw Mr Troll duck his head to squeeze through the door, they banged down their cups and rose from their seats in alarm. The man spilled some coins on the table and they bolted for the door, almost knocking over the Priddles in their haste.

'Well! Really!' said Mrs Priddle.

'Why does everyone run off as soon as we arrive?' asked Ulrik.

'They didn't even finish their lunch,' said Mr Troll. He helped himself to a half-eaten doughnut and licked the sugar off his fingers.

Mrs Troll looked around the empty café. Under a glass case was a tempting display of cakes, pies and tarts, but there was no one to serve them. A coffee machine coughed and gurgled by itself.

'That's funny,' she said. 'There's nobody here.'

'Yes there is,' said Ulrik.

'Where?'

'Over there.' Ulrik dropped his voice to a whisper. 'I think she's playing Hide and Sneak.' He pointed under one of the tables and they all bent down to look. A middle-aged woman in an apron was trying to sneak on her hands and knees towards the kitchen door. Ulrik crept over and bent down until his face was level with hers.

'FOUND YOU!' he cried.

The woman started, banging her head on the table. She crept out and smoothed her apron into place.

'What do you want?' she asked, edging behind the counter rather nervously.

'Four nice creams,' said Mr Troll. 'And Mrs Piddle wants the potty.'

'He means a pot of tea,' said Mrs Priddle, turning pink.

'Yes,' said Mr Troll. 'And what kind of pie is that?' He pointed to the largest one.

'Apple,' said the woman.

'Oh,' said Mr Troll, disappointed. 'I was hoping it might be goat.'

The woman introduced herself as Mrs Evans and brought the tea and ice creams to their table on a tray. After the first shock of seeing the Trolls the colour had returned to her cheeks.

'Gave me a fright you did, walking in like that,' she said. 'I'd just been reading that terrible article in this morning's paper.'

'What article was that?' asked Mr Priddle, pouring his wife some tea.

'You haven't read it?' asked Mrs Evans.

'No.'

'But surely you must have heard?'

'Heard what?' said Mrs Priddle.

'Well . . . about the beast.' Mrs Evans picked up

the *Aberduffy Herald* from the next table and held up the front page for them to see.

'BEAST STRIKES AGAIN!' ran the headline in big bold letters.

Mr Priddle took the paper and started to read. 'Good gravy!' he said, and a moment later, 'Good gracious!'

'For heaven's sake, Roger, what does it say?' cried his wife impatiently.

Mr Priddle read the article out loud. '*Late last night the Beast of Boggy Moor struck again. Eyewitnesses report hearing 'strange sounds' coming from the moor after midnight. A dozen sheep have gone missing bringing the number of attacks this month to four.*'

'Attacks?' gasped Mrs Priddle.

'*Police have appealed for calm,*' her husband went on. '"*We are following a number of lines of inquiry,*" *said Sergeant Morgan of Aberduffy police.* "*Anyone with any information should remember there is a £500 reward for the capture of this beast.*"'

'Wow! Five hundred pounds!' repeated Warren. He exchanged looks with Ulrik, remembering their puzzling conversation with Farmer Ogwen.

No wonder he'd warned them to keep off the moor.

Mrs Priddle had set down her teacup. 'What do you mean by beast?' she asked, nervously. 'What kind of beast?'

'Ah, that nobody knows,' said Mrs Evans, drawing up a chair to sit down. 'No one's ever got close enough to say. There's been several sightings in the last month. All late at night, and all on the moor.'

She lowered her voice and they all leaned closer to listen. 'Mrs Price saw it one night when her car broke down on her way back from Advanced Yoga. There's an evening class in the village hall on—'

'Never mind that! What did she see?' interrupted Mr Priddle.

'Oh yes. Terrified she was. Really shaken up. It passed by not a hundred yards from her car.'

'What was it like?' asked Warren.

'Like a wolf, she said. Or maybe a werewolf – with burning eyes and savage teeth.' She turned to look at Mr Troll. 'In fact a bit like you.'

'Me?'

'Yes,' said Mrs Evans. 'You weren't out on the moor late last night?'

'Don't be silly,' said Mrs Troll. 'We only arrived yesterday and Eggy was asleep with me.'

'That's true. We heard him snoring,' said Mr Priddle.

'Still,' said Mrs Priddle, 'It explains a lot.'

'How do you mean?' asked Mrs Troll.

'Well, that's why people run away when they see you. They think you're this dreadful beast creature.'

'But what about the sheeps?' Ulrik wanted to know.

Mrs Evans looked at him. 'That's the strangest part. You'd think there'd be blood and bones, wouldn't you. But there's never any trace. It's like they've been swallowed whole. A hundred sheep in the last month. I ask you, what kind of beast has that kind of an appetite?' She sat back and smiled pleasantly. 'So how's the tea? Shall I bring you another slice of apple pie?'

Mrs Priddle shook her head. 'Actually,' she said, 'I'm not feeling all that hungry.'

A Darksome Night

THAT EVENING the two families sat in the caravan, talking. It was past eleven o'clock but nobody had mentioned going to bed. The truth was they felt safer in one room. The lamp cast long shadows and the gas fire hissed softly. Steam rose from their mugs of hot chocolate.

'Why didn't Ogwen warn us? That's what I'd like to know,' said Mrs Priddle.

'Maybe he didn't want to alarm us,' suggested her husband.

Ulrik had been thinking back to the morning. 'He did sort of warn us. He told us to keep off the moor, didn't he, Warren?'

'Yes,' agreed Warren, eager to have an opinion. 'But he didn't tell us why. I thought he was just trying to scare us.'

'Huh! He managed that all right,' said Mrs Priddle, bitterly. 'No wonder there are no other caravans. It's hardly a tourist attraction – a wild beast prowling the moor, devouring sheep.

Mr Troll hadn't spoken for a while. He was staring intently out of the window. Suddenly he held up a finger. 'Shhh!'

Everyone fell silent.

'What?' whispered Mr Priddle.

'That noise. Can you hear it?'

They listened again. The caravan rocked slightly. Nobody moved for a full minute.

'What kind of noise?' whispered Mr Priddle at last.

'That strange moaning noise. Like "Ooooooooh! Ooooooooh!"'

'You mean like the wind moaning?'

Mr Troll listened again and his expression relaxed. 'Oh yes, it's only the wind.'

Everyone let out a groan. 'Please don't do that!' said Mrs Priddle, irritably. 'My nerves are on edge as it is. Maybe we should all get to bed.'

Warren shook his head. Now it was dark he wasn't feeling quite so brave.

'What if it comes in the night?' he said. 'What if it tries to get in?'

'I'm sure it won't, Warren. We'll lock the door.'

'But maybe it's a ghost. Ghosts can walk through doors.'

'That's true,' said Mr Troll. 'I once heard of a headless goblin –'

'PLEASE! Don't start on goblins!' shouted Mrs Priddle, banging her mug down on the table.

'Sorry,' said Mr Troll. 'I was only going to say I've got an idea.'

'Oh Lord!' groaned Mr Priddle.

'But I was thinking, why doesn't one of us stay on guard? Then we'll all be safe as mouses.'

'Actually, it's not a bad idea,' admitted Mr Priddle. 'But who's going to stand out there in the dark?' They all looked at each other.

'I will,' said Mr Troll. 'I'm not frighted of hairy beasts.'

Mrs Troll leaned over and gave him a kiss. 'You're my big hairy beast,' she said.

'Well, that's settled then,' said Mrs Priddle. 'Egbert can stay on guard while the rest of us try to get some sleep.'

Ulrik turned to his dad, as the others got ready for bed.

'Dad, can I be on guard with you? I won't be frighted,' he said.

Mr Troll smiled and ruffled his son's hairy head. 'Of course you can, my ugglesome.'

Outside, Mr Troll stamped his feet and blew into his hands to keep warm.

'You stay here, Ulrik, while I go and look for some firewood. A nice roaring fire will keep us warm.'

'Can't I come with you?' asked Ulrik.

'No, somebody's got to stay on guard. I won't be long.'

Ulrik nodded doubtfully.

'Remember, what are trolls?' asked Mr Troll.

'Fierce and scaresome.'

'That's right. And what do trolls do?'

'They roar. Rarrgghh!' growled Ulrik, pulling his fiercest face.

'Not bad,' said Mr Troll, patting him on the head. 'If you hear anything, give a roar and I'll be here in two shakes of a goat's tail. All right?'

Ulrik nodded again. His dad strode off into the darkness in the direction of the woods, leaving him alone. He hugged himself and tromped up and down to keep warm. It was a cold, blustery night with inky clouds racing across the moon. Actually he hadn't told the truth about not feeling scared. With his dad around he felt safe, but he hadn't expected to be left by himself in the dark. Trolls weren't scared of the dark of course but it wasn't the dark that worried him, it was what was *out there* in the dark.

The light in the caravan suddenly went out,

leaving him with only the moon and stars for company. He wished his dad would hurry up with that firewood. How long had he been gone now? The wind gusted and the caravan shuddered on the steep hill. Ulrik tried to think of something to take his mind off being scared. Maybe he could start building the fire. That would impress his dad. He knew the first thing to do was to make a circle of stones or rocks, so the flames wouldn't set light to trees or caravans. Luckily he found just what he needed close at hand. Propped against the wheels of the caravan, he found four heavy rocks. It was almost as if someone had left them there on purpose. Surely no one would mind if he borrowed them for a bit? He began to drag them out one at a time. When he was almost finished something made him look up – the soft thud of footsteps in the dark. They were coming closer.

'Dad?' Ulrik croaked. 'Da-aaad?'

'Baaaa!' said the something. A fat sheep trotted out of the dark, followed a moment later by Mr Troll clutching an armful of sticks.

Before long Ulrik was warming himself in front of a crackling fire. The wood was a little damp, but it soon caught and started to burn. Mr Troll was impressed with the rock circle he'd made.

'Just the jobs,' he said. 'Where did you find them?'

'Under the caravan. Someone must have left them there.'

'I didn't know Piddle collected rocks.'

'Nor did I,' said Ulrik. The gusting wind blew the smoke in his eyes so he had to look away. The caravan groaned and rocked on the hill. It gave a sudden lurch.

'I used to collect rocks when I was your age,' Mr Troll was saying.

'Dad!' said Ulrik, grabbing his arm.

'Me and Snorvik used to swap them –'

'Dad!' interrupted Ulrik. 'The caravan!'

Mr Troll turned round just in time to see the caravan slip past him. It was parked at the top of a steep hill and the slope was taking effect. Slowly at first – like an ocean liner putting out to sea – the caravan began to drift downhill. It swayed and bumped over the grass and picked up a little speed.

Ulrik and Mr Troll chased behind, shouting useful advice like, 'Stop! Come back!' but the caravan took no notice. Even when Ulrik caught up and tried to hang on to the back, it dragged him along until he lost his grip and fell over.

Inside, Mr Priddle had woken with the first sudden jolt. At first he couldn't think where he was, then he remembered he was warm and safe in his caravan. Except that something was wrong. The caravan was bumping and rattling as if it was caught in a force ten gale. Sitting up, he saw the farmhouse drift past the side window. Strange, he thought – farmhouses don't usually do that. Unless . . .

'JACKIE! WARREN! WAKE UP!' he bellowed.

His wife grunted. Warren rolled on to his side.

'We're moving! Wake up!'

Mrs Priddle's eyes blinked open. A glass rolled past her line of vision, followed by the bedside table sliding past. She sat bolt upright.

'Roger! We're moving!' she shouted.

'I know!'

'But how . . .?'

'Never mind how! Let's get out before it's too late.'

Mrs Priddle dragged Warren protesting from the bed. The three of them stumbled and slid in their panic to reach the door. The floor was listing like the deck of a ship in a storm. The fridge door swung open, spilling out milk and eggs and turning the floor into an ice-rink. Warren trod on a gooseberry yoghurt and fell back on the bed which gave a twang and folded beneath him. To add to the confusion, Mrs Troll burst out of her bedroom in her pink nightie, roaring at the top of her voice. The caravan meanwhile hurtled downhill at an alarming speed, its wheels spinning like a custard-coloured Ferrari. Suddenly there was a bang, followed by an almighty splash as it ran out of the field. They bobbed around for a moment listening to bubbling, glugging sounds. Mr Priddle was the first to grasp the situation.

'The pond! We're sinking!' he cried.

'We're going to drown!' wailed Warren.

Mrs Troll pushed past him and wrenched the door open with an effort. A flood of water gushed in over her feet. She grabbed Mrs Priddle by the arm and pulled her to the open door. 'Jump!' she urged.

'Jump! Jump!' cried Mr Priddle.

Mrs Priddle jumped. She landed in cold, murky brown water up to her waist. It was full of weed – and other things. She slopped her way to the bank in her silk pyjamas and sat down among the reeds.

Moments later Ulrik and Mr Troll arrived at the

pond out of breath. Mr Troll took in the rapidly sinking caravan with the water flooding in the door. His wife was wading to the bank carrying Warren piggyback.

Mr Troll shook his head and whistled softly.

'Thank uggness!' he said. 'That could have been nasty.'

A Bit of a Temper

T HEY ALL SPENT the night in the old barn, sleeping on bales of hay. It was draughty, uncomfortable and smelly, with a roof that leaked when it started to rain. At seven o'clock they were woken by Ogwen and his dogs, coming to take the sheep out to the field. Mrs Priddle opened her eyes to find the toothless farmer grinning down at her.

'Morning!' said Ogwen cheerfully. 'I hope you slept well.'

'Not really,' groaned Mrs Priddle. Her back

ached. Everything ached. Her best silk pyjamas were sopping wet. All her dry clothes were in the suitcase, which was in the caravan – which had sunk to the bottom of a filthy pond. It was hard to see how this holiday could get much worse.

The others emerged from the mountain of hay, yawning and dusting themselves down. Farmer Ogwen took in their bedraggled appearance and chuckled.

'Been for a midnight swim, have you?'

'We had a bit of an accident. Our caravan ran away,' explained Mr Priddle.

'I know, I've seen it,' said Ogwen, shaking his head. 'You're going to need a tractor to pull that out. You should have left the brakes on.'

'Yes. Why didn't you, Roger?' asked Mrs Priddle coldly.

'I did. I think they need fixing,' said Mr Priddle. 'But I'm sure I wedged some rocks against the wheels. I remember doing it.'

'Oh,' said Ulrik so loudly that everyone turned to look at him.

'What do you mean, "Oh?"' asked Mr Priddle.

Ulrik looked at his feet sheepishly. He had a feeling he was in trouble.

Later that morning they all gathered around the pond to watch Ogwen attempt to rescue the sunken caravan. The muddy water came up to the bottom of the windows. Ogwen waded in up to his waist, trailing a thick rope behind him. He fished around in the water until he had located the towbar. Once the rope was securely attached, he waded back to the bank, climbed into the cab of his red tractor and revved the engine.

The caravan came out with a loud sucking noise like a hippo emerging from a mud bath. Water gushed out of the door in a brown waterfall, bringing with it a lampshade, three tins of sweetcorn and a soggy toilet roll. Thick, smelly mud oozed off the wheels and clung to the sides.

'It will be fine once we've cleaned it out,' said Mr Priddle hopefully.

'Fine?' said Mrs Priddle. 'FINE?'

'Well, maybe a little damp.'

'Look at it, Roger! It's filthy! It will stink for days.'

Mr Troll stuck his head in between them. 'We don't mind the stink,' he said.

Mrs Priddle gave him a severe look and yanked her husband to one side so they could speak in private. She lowered her voice.

'Roger, I've tried,' she said. 'I've tried to put up with them. But there comes a point when it's asking too much. They'll have to go. Make up your mind – it's either them or me.'

The Trolls stood side by side watching the tractor tow the dripping caravan back up the hill. Mr Priddle approached them and cleared his throat awkwardly.

'Ah, Piddle,' said Mr Troll, turning round. 'Everything's all right then?'

It was the wrong thing to say. Even Mr Troll saw that when Mrs Priddle's eyes bulged like a toad.

'All right?' she burst out. 'All right? You turn up here and ruin our holiday! You sleep in our beds and eat all our food! And, as if that's not enough, last night you tried to drown us!'

'You're having a temper,' observed Mr Troll.

'I know I'm having a temper!' shouted Mrs Priddle.

'That's OK, trolls have tempers. I roar when I'm having a temper. It makes you feel better.'

'I don't want to roar,' glared Mrs Priddle. 'I just want you to take your things and go!'

Mr and Mrs Troll looked at each other and back at the Priddles. 'Go?'

'Yes – go!'

Mrs Troll blinked. 'But we were just starting to enjoy ourselves.'

'In case you hadn't noticed, *I* am not enjoying myself,' said Mrs Priddle. 'I am cold, wet and miserable.'

'And having a temper,' added Mr Troll helpfully.

'But where can we go?' asked Mrs Troll.

'I don't care! Anywhere! Find a hotel, a bus shelter – anything you like as long as it's not near us.'

Mr Troll rubbed his snout. 'So we're not on holidays any more?'

'Not with us you're not!' thundered Mrs Priddle, and stalked off up the hill with her husband following meekly behind. The Trolls stared after them, at a loss.

'Well! For uggness' sake!' sighed Mrs Troll.

'Yes,' agreed Mr Troll. 'Fancy getting all hot and blethered over a tiddly bit of water.'

'It was quite a lot of water,' admitted Mrs Troll. 'But you know what peeples are like.' Her husband nodded. 'Mad as a sack of goblins.'

'And just when I thought we were all getting on so well,' said Mrs Troll. 'What are we going to do now, Eggy? Where are we going to sleep tonight?'

Mr Troll frowned. 'I don't know. Where's Ulrik?'

They looked around. There was no sign of him. Warren stood with his back to the barn and his hands covering his eyes. He seemed to be counting to himself.

'Ahh! They're playing a game!' said Mrs Troll. 'Why don't we leave them, Eggy? There's no sense in upsetting Ulrik now. We can come back for him once we've found somewheres to sleep.'

'All right,' agreed Mr Troll. 'You think there might be caves?'

'You never know.'

'Come on, my lugly.'

Mr Troll took his wife's hand and together they set off towards the village.

Hide and Sneak

'. . . **F**ORTY-NINE, fifty!' Warren opened his eyes. Actually, he hadn't kept them fully closed. He'd been peeking through his fingers the whole time in order to see where Ulrik went. Just as he suspected, Ulrik had made a beeline for the woods, since there wasn't really anywhere else on the farm to hide. It wouldn't take long to find him, though Warren wasn't in a tearing hurry. The woods were dark and they backed on to Boggy Moor. Warren wasn't scared himself, of course. All the same, as he entered the woods, he stopped to arm himself with a big stick.

He followed a rough, muddy path and eventually came to a wide clearing overgrown with ferns. Looking around, he half expected to see Ulrik's large hairy head or his bottom poking out from behind one of the trees. There was no sign of him. Warren went on, swishing at the tops of the ferns with his stick. *Swish!* Ogwen had warned them to stay out of the woods, he recalled. There wasn't anything to worry about, of course – the beast only came out after dark. *Swish, swish!* Though you could never be certain. It might be here watching him right now.

He halted and glanced around nervously. Maybe if he hadn't stopped he wouldn't have noticed the odd way the ferns lay on the ground ahead of him – as if someone had arranged them deliberately. He prodded one aside with his stick. Underneath was a piece of chicken wire and beneath that a dark, yawning hole. Warren squatted down to examine it more closely. It was some kind of animal trap and if he'd taken a couple more steps he would have fallen right into it! But why would someone dig a hole in the middle of the woods? It was far too big for catching rabbits and he hadn't come across any other wild animals.

The words in yesterday's paper jumped into his mind – '£500 reward for catching the beast'. So that was it! – someone was after the reward! Warren almost wished he'd thought of the idea himself. Five hundred pounds was a lot of pocket money – think of all the sweets and ice creams he could buy with that! He pictured his photo on the front page of tomorrow's paper and his name in the headlines. 'Warren the beast-slayer' they'd call him.

Of course it was only a daydream. He was never going to catch the beast or get his hands on the reward . . . unless . . . A sly smile spread across Warren's face. Nobody actually knew what the beast looked like, did they?

Carefully, he replaced the ferns so that the hole was hidden from sight. Once he was satisfied, he stood up and raised his hands to his mouth.

'ULRIK! Ulrik, over here!'

Ulrik meanwhile was getting tired of hiding. He'd

been crouching in the middle of a prickly bush for what felt like hours. One of his feet had gone to sleep. Maybe Warren had given up looking for him altogether. Maybe he was too scared to come into the woods. He pricked up his ears. Someone was shouting his name.

He followed the voice until he came to a wide clearing, where he found Warren waiting for him.

'Why didn't you come to find me?' he asked.

Warren shrugged. 'I've been looking. You're too good at hiding.'

Ulrik looked pleased. 'Really? Does that mean I winned the game?'

'Yep, you won. Come on, let's go back now.' Warren sounded impatient.

'But isn't it your turn to hide?' asked Ulrik.

Warren glanced down. One more step. 'What?' he said.

'I said, "Isn't it your turn?"'

'No! The game's over. Hurry up!'

'Oh. I thought . . .' But Ulrik never got to say what he thought because he took another step towards Warren and suddenly the ground gave way beneath his feet. He fell into the trap, with branches and ferns crashing down on top of him.

For a moment he lay still, more dazed than hurt.

'What happened?' he groaned.

Warren peered down at him. 'Looks like you fell in a hole.'

Ulrik scrambled to his feet. He'd bruised his knee. The hole was so deep that even standing on tiptoe he couldn't reach the top. He stretched up a hand to Warren.

'Help me out!'

Warren shook his head. 'I can't.'

'Warren!'

'Sorry, you're too heavy. You weigh a ton. If I try to pull you out I'll probably end up falling in with you. Then we'll both be stuck.'

Ulrik blinked up at him. It was true, he was bigger and heavier than Warren.

'What are we going to do?' he asked anxiously.

'Don't worry, you stay there. I'll go and fetch help.'

'Wait!' called Ulrik. 'You're not going to leave me all by myself?'

'It won't be for long. I'll run back to the caravan

and tell them what's happened. Five minutes and I'll be back again.'

'You promise?'

'Scout's honour,' said Warren, raising a hand in salute. He gave Ulrik a cheery wave and walked away, smiling secretly to himself. Of course he had never been in the Scouts, but Ulrik didn't know that.

Missing Ulrik

BACK AT THE farm, Mr Priddle was doing his best to clean out the waterlogged caravan.

He squeezed muddy brown water from his mop into a bucket. His wife and son were refusing to help – Mrs Priddle said they were on strike. She looked up from the novel she was reading and shook her head.

'I don't know why you're wasting time on that, Roger.'

'The floor's almost dry,' said her husband.

'I've told you, I'm not sleeping in there.'

'You'll get used to the smell after a while.'

'I don't want to get used to it. I want to move to a nice hotel.'

Warren stopped juggling with his football. 'Will the hotel have a swimming pool?' he asked.

'Of course it will, my poppet,' said Mrs Priddle.

Mr Priddle thumped his mop on the floor. 'We're not going to any hotel, we're staying here! I've paid Ogwen for two weeks!'

'Fine. You stay in your smelly old caravan if you like, Roger; we're not,' said Mrs Priddle, placidly turning her page.

Mr Priddle emptied a bucketful of brown water into the grass.

'The sun's shining, you're out in the fresh air, what more do you want?'

Mrs Priddle gave him a withering look. 'Dry clothes,' she said.

'Can I have cooked breakfast at the hotel?' asked Warren.

'Have what you like, darling, your father's paying,' said Mrs Priddle.

'Will the Trolls be coming too?'

'No,' said Mrs Priddle firmly. 'They're having their own holiday.'

'Where?' asked Warren.

'I've no idea. That's up to them.'

Warren glanced anxiously back at the woods. It was hours since he'd left Ulrik and set off towards town with the intention of claiming the £500 reward. But the closer he got to the village, the more he'd begun to lose faith in his plan. For one thing, he wasn't exactly sure where the police station was. For another, he doubted the police would believe a word of his story. Hairy and ugly he might be, but Ulrik didn't sound much like a savage beast once he opened his mouth. He was far too gentle and good-natured. Even worse, Warren thought, what if Mr and Mrs Troll discovered that he'd tried to swap their son for £500? Warren had seen Mr Troll in a temper and he didn't wish to be picked up and swung round by his ears. No, he'd decided in the end, it would never work. Far safer to go back and just keep quiet.

When he returned to the caravan his parents were too busy arguing to even notice that Ulrik was missing. All the same, Warren was starting to feel uneasy. What if Ulrik never got out of the hole? What if he stayed there for ever and starved to death? Come to think of it, Warren was pretty hungry himself. Wasn't it time for supper?

His dad carried a bundle of soggy sheets from the caravan and began to peg them on a washing line.

'I wonder where they are,' he pondered.

'Who?' asked his wife.

'The Trolls. They've been gone hours. You think they're all right?'

'All right?' snorted Mrs Priddle. 'They're trolls, Roger, not children!'

'Yes,' said Mr Priddle. 'That's what worries me.'

Mr and Mrs Troll's search for somewhere to stay was not going well. As soon as the villagers saw them coming down the hill they scurried into their houses and locked their doors. Mrs Troll spotted a sign in the window of a tall white house offering 'Bed and Breakfast', but when she knocked on the door a hand appeared and turned the sign around so that it said 'No Vacancies'.

'Now what?' she asked her husband.

Mr Troll pointed down the hill to a van parked by a playground.

'Look! There's a caravan just like the Piddles'.'

When they got closer they found the caravan was empty. It was bright pink, and for reasons Mr Troll didn't fully grasp it had a giant ice-cream cornet parked on the roof. People's strange ideas never ceased to amaze him. He peered in through the window. 'It's a bit tiddly,' he said, 'but we could all squish up on the floor.'

'I don't know, Eggy,' said Mrs Troll doubtfully. 'Doesn't it belong to someone? Maybe we should ask.'

Mr Troll looked up and down the deserted village street. 'Who can we ask? Come on, they won't mind if we take a look. Give me a legs-up.'

Mrs Troll panted and pushed him from behind while her husband struggled to squeeze his bulky frame through the narrow window.

'Push harder!' said Mr Troll. 'My bottoms are stuck!'

'I am pushing harder! You've put on weight!'

'One more shove!'

Mrs Troll summoned all her strength and gave one

last shove. It did the trick and Mr Troll fell head-first into the van, grabbing at a lever to try and break his fall. A large blob of ice cream oozed from a nozzle. It hung for a moment and then landed neatly on top of his head. He scrambled to his feet.

Mrs Troll stared at him. 'A bird's plopped on your head.'

Mr Troll dabbed at the blob with a finger and tasted it. 'That's not bird-plop, it's nice cream,' he said. 'Ulrik will love this – a caravan with its own nice cream.'

He set about heaving his wife in through the window and the two of them inspected their new lodgings.

'It's much tiddlier than the Piddles',' said Mrs Troll. 'Where's the folding bed?'

She opened a door. A blast of cold air hit her in the face and mist billowed out. 'It's full of lollies,' she said.

"Scuse me!'

A shrill voice brought Mr Troll to the window. A small, curly-haired girl was staring up at him, holding out a coin.

'A Ninety-nine, please, mister,' she said.

'Pardon?' replied Mr Troll.

'A Ninety-nine. With a chocolate flake.'

Mr Troll turned to his wife. 'She wants ninety-nine chocolate cakes.'

'We haven't got any cakes.'

'I know. Maybe she'll take a nice cream instead.'

'Wait there,' he told the little girl. He examined

the ice-cream machine and pulled down the lever. A large blob of whipped vanilla plopped on to the floor between his feet. Mr Troll tried again and managed to catch the next blob on his right foot. He looked around for a bowl or plate but there didn't seem to be any. Instead he raised his foot and propped it carefully on the counter. 'There we are. One nice cream,' he said. 'You'll have to lick it off.' The little girl frowned back at him.

Just then a voice made them look up. A man was running down the hill towards them at high speed, his white coat flapping behind him.

'Hoi!' he shouted crossly. 'What do you think you're doing?'

'Bogles!' muttered Mr Troll.

'I told you we should have asked,' said Mrs Troll.

'That's my van! Get out of there!' bellowed the man.

'I think it's his caravan,' sighed Mr Troll.

'Yes,' said Mrs Troll. 'And it doesn't look like he wants us to stay.'

Half an hour later the Trolls arrived back at the

farm. By now the sun was low in the sky and the shadows were lengthening. They had spent most of the day tramping the road between the village and Sunny Bay. Now they were returning, weary and homeless. 'What are we going to tell Ulrik?' asked Mrs Troll gloomily.

Mr Troll shrugged. 'Maybe the Piddles will have changed their mind. Maybe they'll let us sleep with them tonight.'

Mrs Troll shook her head. 'I don't think so. Mrs Piddle was having a big temper.'

'Yes,' agreed Mr Troll. 'Peeples look funny when they're having a temper. Their faces go red as tomatoes. Does mine do that?'

'No my lugly, it stays green.'

They found the Priddles by their caravan. Mr Priddle had dragged all the mattresses outside and was attempting to dry off the damp patches with a hairdryer. Mrs Priddle watched him with her arms folded and an impatient expression on her face. She didn't seem overjoyed to see the Trolls back again.

'Well?' she said.

'We tried everywhere,' said Mrs Troll. 'No one wants us to stay.'

'I can't say I blame them,' said Mrs Priddle.

Mrs Troll looked around. 'Where's Ulrik?'

'Ulrik?' Mr Priddle blinked in surprise. 'I thought he was with you.'

'No,' said Mrs Troll. 'We left him with you. He was playing with Warren.'

They all turned to look at Warren, whose cheeks had gone so red that Mr Troll wondered if he was having a temper.

'Warren? Have you seen Ulrik?' asked Mrs Priddle.

'Um . . . well, I saw him a while ago,' admitted Warren. 'But then he went off.'

'Off? Off where, for uggness' sake?' demanded Mr Troll.

Warren avoided his gaze. 'I don't know. He didn't really say.'

Mrs Troll looked at Mr Troll. 'Oh Eggy! That's not like Ulrik to go off without telling anyone. What if he's lost? What if something's happened?'

'Now, now, let's all try to stay calm,' said Mr Troll, tromping up and down and looking anything but calm.

Mrs Priddle turned to her son. 'Warren, try to remember. This is important. Which way did Ulrik go?'

Warren bit his lip. If he said the woods, they would find Ulrik trapped in the hole and everyone would blame him. Better to put them off the scent. He frowned, pretending to think, then pointed up the hill.

'That way.'

Mrs Troll clasped a hand to her mouth. 'Eggy! The moor! He's out on the moor!'

Troll in the Hole

ULRICK HUGGED HIS knees and shivered. Darkness was closing in and he could see the moon pale as a ghost overhead. He'd lost track of how long he'd been trapped in the hole. At first he'd thought it was only a matter of time before his mum or dad would come and find him, but hours had passed and no rescue had come. Surely by now Warren would have told them what had happened?

He'd given up trying to escape – the hole was too deep and the sides too muddy and slippery to climb out. His voice was hoarse from shouting for help. All he could do was wait and hope that someone would find him. He hummed to himself, trying to remember a trollaby* his mum used to sing to him as a troggler. Mrs Evans had said the beast came out after dark. Surely it wouldn't want to eat a plump young troll? Sheeps were much more tastesome. Abruptly he stopped humming. Had he imagined it? That awful howl carried on the wind. He listened. A second howl split the night air, this time longer and louder than the first.

Ulrik tried not to panic. If he stayed where he was maybe the beast would pass by. But what if it didn't? What if it smelt him out? Dogs could pick up your smell and maybe beasts were the same. He reached up, making one last desperate attempt to escape. His fingers touched something hard and he grabbed at it. Warren's stick fell into the hole at his feet.

---

* *Trollaby – soft crooning song, often about hunting goats.*

Half a mile away, Mr Troll climbed on top of a rock and cupped his hands to his mouth. 'ULRIK!' he roared. 'Ul-rik!'

There was no answer. Mr Priddle shone his torch into the dark.

'It's no use,' he said. 'We'll never find him out here.'

The moor seemed to be endless. Craggy rocks loomed in the dark like giants and solid ground gave way to boggy marsh that squelched under their feet. Mrs Troll blew her snout loudly on her hanky. 'My poor little Ulrik!' she sniffed.

Warren dug his hands in his pockets and shivered. 'Can't we go back now?' he begged. 'There's nothing out here.'

'You go back if you're frighted,' said Mr Troll. 'I'm not giving up till I find him.'

'Nor me,' said Mrs Troll. But before they could go on they heard a sound that chilled them to the bone. It was the same blood-curdling howl that Ulrik had heard in the woods.

'Jumping goblins!' said Mr Troll.

'That's not a goblin,' said Mr Priddle. 'It's some kind of animal. It came from the woods.'

A low moan escaped Warren.

Mr Priddle shone his torch on his son's face, which had gone deathly white.

'It was only a joke,' Warren stammered. 'I thought he'd be all right. I never meant . . .'

'What the bogles is he blethering about?' growled Mr Troll.

'Ulrik . . .' babbled Warren. 'He fell down a hole in the woods. It was an accident!'

'What?' said Mr Priddle. 'Why on earth didn't you say this before?'

Warren whimpered. 'I thought you'd be cross!'

'I am cross!' shouted Mr Priddle.

'I'm double cross!' roared Mr Troll. 'I'm cross as a hot cross bun!'

Before anyone could stop him he seized Warren and dangled him upside down by one leg.

'Arghhhhh!' shrieked Warren. 'Daaad!'

'For uggness' sake, Eggy, put him down!' scolded Mrs Troll. 'It's Ulrik we need to worry about. He's all alone in that wood with a scaresome beast!'

'By the bogles, you're right!' said Mr Troll, dropping Warren in a puddle. 'We've got to find Ulrik before it's too late! Come on!'

He set off, bounding towards the woods at great speed with the others trying to keep up.

Beastly!

BACK IN THE hole, Ulrik was certain the beast could smell him. Just now he'd glimpsed a pair of huge yellow eyes moving through the trees like searchlights. A menacing growl made his hair stand on end and reminded him that he wanted to go to the toilet. He gripped his stick tightly. If the beast came at him, he decided, he'd poke it in the eye. Or maybe it would be better to throw the stick and shout 'Fetch!' – he'd seen that work on a dog once.

A rustle in the trees told him the beast was

approaching. He shrank back in the shadows of the hole. Heavy footsteps came closer. Whatever it was, it was big enough to make the ground shake. A shadow loomed over him and a bright light dazzled his eyes. Ulrik jabbed upwards with his stick.

'Owwww!' yelped Mr Priddle.

'Ulrik?' said a familiar voice. 'Is that you?'

'Dad!' cried Ulrik.

Mr Troll's strong arms reached down and caught hold of him, lifting him out.

His mum wiped away a tear and hugged him so tightly he could hardly breathe.

'Thank uggness! Are you all right, my ugglesome?'

'I'm fine,' said Ulrik.

'He poked me in the eye!' complained Mr Priddle.

'Sorry, I thought you were the beast,' said Ulrik. 'I heard it!'

As if on cue another growl came from the moor.

'Good gravy!' gasped Mr Priddle, forgetting his sore eye. 'That sounded close!'

Warren tugged at his dad's sleeve.

'Let's go back!' he begged. 'Mum will be getting worried.'

Ulrik held up a hand for silence. 'Listen!' he said.

They all heard it – a faint bleating carried on the wind.

'Sheeps,' said Mr Troll.

Warren panicked. 'It's coming for them!' he trembled. 'It's after the sheeps – I mean sheep.'

'But Dad,' said Ulrik, 'we can't just leave them. They'll be eaten by the beast.'

'They won't be the only ones if we don't get out of here,' muttered Mr Priddle.

But he was talking to himself – the trolls were already creeping forward through the trees towards the moor and whatever was out there.

Ulrik peered out from behind a tree at the edge of the woods. He could see the beast's dark head over the top of a stone wall. His mum and dad stole forward to join him.

'Ready?' whispered Mr Troll.

Ulrik and Mrs Troll nodded.

'No roaring,' hissed Mr Troll. 'Let's take it by surprises.'

'You're the one who's always roaring,' said Mrs Troll sniffily.

'Shhh!' said Ulrik, gripping his stick.

'After three,' said Mr Troll. 'One, two, three . . .'

The Trolls came running and bounding out of the wood and threw themselves on top of the beast. Ulrik leapt on its back and grabbed it around the neck. It toppled over limply.

Something funny had happened to its growls, which sounded like someone gargling underwater. Ulrik let go and sat up, staring in surprise.

'Good goblins!' said Mr Troll. 'It's just a dog.'

The black Labrador lay on its side, staring ahead with glassy eyes. It had been stuffed and mounted on wheels like a pull-along toy. Under the dog's belly were two speakers from which came the deafening growls and howls they'd heard earlier. Someone, it seemed, had been playing a trick.

A hundred yards down the slope, the headlights of a truck lit up the moor. Ulrik recognised the pair of yellow eyes he thought he'd seen from the woods. The driver turned off the engine and got out, closing the door. Even from this distance Ulrik recognised the baggy trousers and shabby coat.

'Look! It's Ogwen!' he whispered.

'Good Gravy! So it is!' Now the fighting was over, the Priddles had crept forward to join them. The five of them crouched in the dark to watch. Ogwen put his fingers to his mouth and whistled to his dogs. Fang and Claw were rounding up a small flock of confused-looking sheep and chasing them towards the back of the truck. In a few minutes the farmer had them all inside and the tailgate bolted shut. Ogwen gave another shrill whistle, calling in his dogs.

'I don't believe it,' hissed Mr Priddle. 'He's a rustler!'

'A wrestler?' Mr Troll looked puzzled.

'He's stealing them, Dad. They're not his sheep,' explained Ulrik.

'Great goblins! You mean he's a robber?'

'Yes!'

Mr Troll bunched his fists and rose to his feet. There was nothing he hated more than robbers. 'Wait till I catch him!' he threatened. 'I'll tromp on his bellies. I'll swing him by the uncles!'

Ulrik pulled him back. 'Wait, Dad. I've got a better idea.'

'Better than tromping?'

'Yes. Let's see how *he* likes getting a fright.'

Ogwen closed the door of his truck and grinned toothlessly.

He was pleased with his night's work. Twenty-three more sheep to add to his growing flock. At this rate he'd soon be the richest farmer in Aberduffy.

He returned to the edge of the woods, where he'd left Bessie. It was amazing what you could do with a stuffed dog and a few sound effects. At the edge of the woods he stopped and looked around, baffled. The dog had gone! Vanished! But that was impossible – how could it walk off by itself?

'Grarrgghh!' A loud roar from the darkness startled him. It wasn't like the growls and howls on the tape – this sounded all too real and alive.

'Who's there?' he asked, trying to steady his quavering voice.

The reply was close to a second roar, this time the truck. His escape was cut off. Ogwen backed away towards the trees, trembling. There was more than one of them – maybe a whole pack of wolves or bears closing in on him.

'GRARRGH!' The next roar was so loud he yelped and crashed through the woods, ducking under branches. Scratched and panting, he came out into a clearing. Something was standing there waiting for him. When he got closer he saw it was Bessie, her glassy eyes shining in the dark.

'Bessie?' he said uncertainly.

'Grrrrrr!' replied the dog. Ogwen's mouth gaped open.

'Bessie? Is that you, girl?'

'Grrrrrr – robber – grrrrr!'

Ogwen pinched himself. Was he dreaming? The dog had spoken to him, calling him a robber. But Bessie had died five years ago. Maybe it was her ghost come back to haunt him.

'Bessie, it's me, Olwen! It's master!'

He reached out a hand cautiously . . .

'GRARGHHH!' roared Ulrik, leaping out from behind the dog.

'Arghhhhhh!' yelled Ogwen as the ground gave way and he fell back into the deep muddy hole.

When he came to his senses, he saw three hairy trolls grinning down at him from above.

'We'll done, Ulrik!' said Mr Troll. 'That was fun!'

'Did I make a good dog? Grrrr!' said Ulrik, showing his fangs.

Mrs Troll patted him proudly on the head. 'You were scaresome, my hairling.'

A short time afterwards Sergeant Morgan arrived from the local police station.

'Hello?' he said, shining his torch. 'I heard there was some trouble. We had a call from a Mrs Puddle.'

'Priddle,' said Mr Priddle wearily.

'Pardon?'

'Priddle. That's my name.'

'Oh. Who's this in the hole then?' He shone his torch on the miserable face of Ogwen.

'Olwen Ogwen. Well, well! What are you doing down there?'

'He's a robber,' Mr Troll informed the sergeant. 'He's been wrestling sheep.'

'Wrestling them?'

'He means rustling,' explained Mr Priddle. 'If you look on the moor you'll find his truck. The stolen sheep are in the back.'

'And this, said Ulrik, 'is the beast of Boggy Moor.' He trundled Bessie forward so that the policeman could see her and switched on the tape. Growls and howls came from the two speakers. Sergeant Morgan took off his cap and scratched his head.

'Well I'll be jiggered! So that's what it was! The

chief's going to be pleased about this. Very pleased. We've been trying to get to the bottom of this for months. Of course I never believed in all this beast nonsense myself.'

'Didn't you?' asked Mr Priddle.

'Oh no, not for a moment. "Someone's leading us a merry dance" – that's what I said to the chief. But fancy it turning out to be Olwen Ogwen all the time! There'll be a reward for this, you know.'

Mr Priddle's face brightened. 'A reward? Goodness! I had no idea.'

He felt a large hairy hand on his shoulder. 'Ahem!' growled Mr Troll.

'Oh well, yes,' said Mr Priddle hastily. 'Strictly speaking it was Ulrik who did most of the work.'

Ulrik smiled shyly as the Sergeant shook him firmly by the hand.

'Good work, young Ulrik. You come by the station and we'll see about that five hundred pounds, shall we?'

'Uggsome!' said Ulrik.

A loud groan made them all look round. 'Are you OK, Warren?' asked Ulrik. 'You've gone a bit green.'

Wish you were Here!

MRS PRIDDLE LAY on her sunbed and sipped her fruit cocktail through a straw. The ice cubes clinked soothingly against the glass. Below her balcony she could hear children laughing and playing happily in the hotel swimming pool. Warren's shrill voice rang out above the hubbub. 'Mum! Watch me!'

Mrs Priddle waved back at him. 'Lovely, darling! Well done!'

She sighed deeply – at last a proper holiday! The strange events of the previous night seemed like a dream. In any case, everything had worked out well. After hours of tramping the moor, Mr Priddle was ready to abandon his damp caravan and move into a comfortable hotel. She glanced at him now, lying on the sunbed next to hers.

'So there never was any beast at all?' she said.

'Mmm? No. I told you, Ogwen invented the whole thing just to keep people off the moor at night.'

'But what about the story in the paper? People claimed they saw it.'

Mr Priddle chuckled. 'It just shows you the power of the imagination. Tell people there's a savage beast on the moor and that's what they believe. Actually, it was nothing more than a stuffed dog – Ogwen's favourite Labrador, Bessie. It seems he couldn't bear to be parted from her.'

'Heavens! He sounds a total fruitcake,' remarked Mrs Priddle.

'I'm afraid so. I heard him tell the police the dog had come back to haunt him.'

Mrs Priddle shook her head. She had never trusted the farmer from the start – you could tell he didn't clean his teeth properly.

'Well, thank goodness it's all over,' she said. 'No more sleepless nights, no more caravans, and best of all, no more trolls.'

'Bliss!' agreed Mr Priddle.

Mrs Priddle closed her eyes, hoping to doze off. She could hear seagulls calling and the *put-put* of a car coming slowly along the road. In fact it wasn't a car, it was more like . . .

'Oh good gravy!' said Mr Priddle, sitting bolt upright.

'What?'

'That's our caravan!'

'Don't be ridiculous, Roger. We left it back at the farm.'

'It is, and it's turning in here!'

Mrs Priddle's eyes snapped open and she jumped to her feet. Below her balcony she could see a large red tractor turning into the drive. At the wheel was Mr Troll, who had never driven a tractor before but was obviously enjoying the experience. He was towing the Priddles' battered old caravan behind and Ulrik and Mrs Troll could be seen hanging out of the windows.

'Oh no!' groaned Mrs Priddle. She tried to hide

but it was too late – Mr Troll had spotted them and waved excitedly.

'Piddle! Look what I've got. We've cleaned it up for you!'

'Cleaned it up?' Mrs Priddle turned pale. She dared not think what that meant.

Mr Priddle waved his arms. 'No! We don't want it! Go away!'

'What?' asked Mr Troll, putting a hand to his ear and forgetting to steer. The tractor swerved violently to the left.

'I said . . . look out!' shouted Mr Priddle.

The tractor ploughed straight across the Hotel Majestic's lawn, leaving deep muddy tracks in its wake. It was heading directly for the swimming pool. Sunbathers ran for cover, scattering in all directions. A waiter dropped his tray of drinks and vaulted a sunbed faster than an Olympic hurdler. The pool was emptying fast.

'Brakes!' bellowed Mr Priddle. 'Use the brakes!'

'Which one is brakes?' Mr Troll called back. He had only just learned how to make the tractor go forward – stopping it was another matter. He chose a lever at random and pushed it, jamming his foot down on one of the pedals. The tractor leapt forward like a startled kangaroo. The Priddles shut their eyes, unable to watch. When it came, the splash was so enormous it drenched them five floors up.

Bubbling and hissing, the tractor went down in the deep end, dragging the caravan in with it. A moment later Ulrik bobbed to the surface, followed by Mr and Mrs Troll. They struggled to the side of the pool, where a crowd of spectators had gathered to watch.

Ulrik climbed up the steps and sat down.

'Mum! Did you see me? I swimmed!'

'Well done, my ugglesome!'

The manager of the Majestic pushed his way through the crowd, crimson with rage.

'Is this your caravan?' he demanded, pointing to the sunken wreck.

The Trolls looked at each other. 'Well, no,' said Mr Troll. 'It isn't.'

'Then whose is it?'

'It's the Piddles'.'

Mr Troll pointed to the balcony – but strangely enough there was no sign of the Priddles at all.